GHOST STORIES

Illustrated by
Walt Sturrock

The Unicorn Publishing House, Inc.
New Jersey

The Legend of Sleepy Hollow

From The Story By Washington Irving

In the great State of New York, in one of the many little retired Dutch valleys, is a small town known as Sleepy Hollow. Though many years have passed since I have ridden through the drowsy shades of Sleepy Hollow, I still have fresh memories of a peculiar incident that was related to me so long ago.

In this remote little village lived a schoolmaster by the name of Ichabod Crane. He had come recently to town from his home in Connecticut to run the local school-house. He was tall, exceedingly thin, with narrow shoulders and long arms and legs. His hands dangled a mile out of his sleeves and his feet could have well served for shovels as they were so large and flat. His head was small, and flat on top, with huge ears, large green glassy eyes, and a long pointed nose. To see him walking along a hill on a windy day, one might mistake him for a scarecrow who was running away from his job in the cornfield.

His school-house was a low building of one large room, rudely made of logs. It stood in a rather lonely but pleasant spot, just at the foot of a woody hill, with a brook running close by.

As a schoolmaster it could be said he never spared the rod and spoiled the child, but neither was he a cruel teacher. However, it could be said his lessons were particularly dry and dull, and his style was never such as to be inspiring to any of his pupils. He was in a word a bore.

On Sundays he led the church choir in song, and by all accounts was a pious, levelheaded young man.

If it could be said Ichabod Crane had any great shortcomings, it might be his appetite for the strange and mysterious. He often pored over one curious book, Cotton Mather's *History of New England Witchcraft,* of which he firmly believed every single word. He was entranced by the tales of woe and misery the evil witches brought upon their hapless victims. The midnight rituals, riding of broomsticks, stealing babies from their cradles—all these things Ichabod believed happened—and he delighted in reading about them. He could often be seen climbing upon the hills with his nose stuffed between the pages, greedily taking in every witch, black cat, and dark curse that man has had to endure.

The effect of all these horrible tales was evident. Ichabod was very high strung and his imagination was overly excited. The moan of a whippoorwill from the hill-side, the ominous cry of the tree toad, the hooting of a screech owl, or the sudden rustle in the thicket of birds could set Ichabod to trembling and longing for the fastest way home. On many a fall evening, a firefly suddenly lighting up in his path, or a beetle flying across his face, would send him flying through the wood in fright. Ichabod was in many ways a coward. But still he loved to read and reread the dire tales of black witches and of things that go bump in the night.

When fearing for his safety from some dark fiend or spirit, his only recourse to drive away the evil was to sing psalm-tunes. The good people of Sleepy Hollow, as they sat by their doors in the evening, were often filled with awe, hearing his nasal melody floating from a distant hill, or along the dusky road.

Another of his sources of fearful pleasure was to pass the long winter evenings with the old Dutch wives. As they sat spinning by the fire, with a row of apples roasting and spluttering along the hearth, Ichabod would delight them with tales of haunted

fields, and haunted brooks, and haunted bridges, and haunted houses. He would thrill them with stories of ghosts and goblins, and in particular of the headless horseman, or the Galloping Hessian of the Hollow, as they sometimes called him. He would frighten them terribly with talk of comets and shooting-stars colliding with the earth, and the alarming fact that the world turned around, and that they were half the time topsy-turvy!

But if there was a pleasure in all this, while snug and warm by the fire, it was dearly bought by the terrors of his lonely walks back home. What fearful shapes and shadows beset his path amid the dim and ghastly glare of a snowy night! With wild fancy he looked at every trembling ray of light streaming across the white fields. How often was he appalled by some shrub covered with snow, which, like some ghostly ghoul, beset his every path! He would shrink in terror at the sound of his own steps on the frosty crust beneath his feet. He dreaded to look back over his shoulder lest he behold some fiend tramping close behind him! Ichabod was especially fearful when a sudden blast of wind would send the trees howling, as he fancied that the Galloping Hessian was riding down upon him!

All these, however, were mere terrors of the night, phantoms of the mind that walk in darkness. Daylight put an end to all these evils; and he would have passed a pleasant life of it, despite the devil and all his works, except for one thing. Ichabod's path was soon crossed by a being more confusing to mortal man than ghosts, goblins, and the whole race of witches put together, that is—a woman.

Among the members of the choir that assembled one evening every week to be instructed by Ichabod was Katrina Van Tassel, the daughter of a rich Dutch farmer. She was a lovely girl of eighteen; plump as a partridge, ripe and melting and rosy-cheeked as a peach, and full of expectations for her life; indeed for the world at large.

She was more than a bit of a flirt with the young men, so needless to say it wasn't long before poor Ichabod's head was turned. He had a soft and foolish heart toward women, and this became especially true with regard to the youthful Katrina after he laid his eyes on her father's estate. A lowly schoolmaster, too, does not live by bread alone. Nor his books for that matter.

But there were other rivals for the fair hand of Katrina, most formidable of all being a burly fellow by the name of Brom Bones. Brom was big and broad-shouldered, with short, curly dark hair. He had rough but not unhandsome features, having a mingling air of fun and arrogance about him. He was known as a man with a good sense of humor if not downright mischief. But he was a simpler, more straightforward fellow than Ichabod, and this proved a disadvantage in courting the flighty Katrina.

Under cover of his character as singing-master, Ichabod was able to make frequent trips to visit Katrina on her father's farm. In addition, he was well-read and could speak of worldly things, of faraway things that tend to turn a young girl's head.

At town dances, Ichabod would usually have the greater share of attention from the fair Katrina, forcing Brom to sit helplessly and watch in frustration. Ichabod was simply in heaven, and in many ways was becoming bigheaded. After all, he thought, who was more deserving than himself to win the hand of the rich and beautiful Katrina? The other suitors, to his mind, were far too simple and brutish for such a delicate creature. And many in the town of Sleepy Hollow agreed, after seeing the two together, that it was only a matter of time before wedding bells would ring.

Now it happened one fall evening, after a dance, that the men gathered and told stories. Many of the old Dutchmen told seafaring tales, but of all the stories told that night, Ichabod's ghost stories, especially that of the headless horseman, were the most welcome to the listeners. Brom, more put out than ever, left early that evening.

Ichabod told half a dozen ghost stories, with great effect, before deciding it was time to head for home. Ichabod set off slowly down the dark road on his horse, old Gunpowder.

In the shadow of a grove, by the side of a little brook, Ichabod saw something that made the hairs stand on his neck. He beheld something huge, misshapen, black, and towering. What was to be done? To turn and fly was now too late; and besides, what chance was there of escaping ghost or goblin? Summoning up a show of courage, he demanded in a trembling voice, "Who are you?" He received no reply. He repeated his demand with greater agitation. In reply, the thing began to climb slowly up a small hill. Ichabod could see now that it appeared to be a horseman who was mounted upon a black horse of powerful frame. Ichabod did not call out again, but spurred old Gunpowder to move on. He did, however, turn around to see if the horseman was moving off away from him as well. Ichabod was horror-struck. The horseman was atop the small hill, which brought him in relief against the night sky. Ichabod could plainly see that the rider was headless! But his horror was still greater on observing that the head, which should have rested atop the shoulders, was carried before the rider on his saddle.

Ichabod rained a shower of kicks and blows upon Gunpowder, hoping, by a sudden movement, to give the ghoul the slip. Away then they dashed, stones flying and sparks flashing at every bound. But to Ichabod's dismay, the headless horseman was in full pursuit and getting closer with each stride.

The road led through a sandy hollow, shaded by trees for about a quarter of a mile, where it then crossed a bridge over a very dark and deep brook. Just beyond the bridge lay the town church. Ichabod remembered through his terror the story of the headless horseman he had told the old gentlemen that very night. As legend went, the goblin could not cross over the church bridge. If the horseman did try to cross the bridge, he

would instantly vanish in a blaze of fire and brimstone.

Ichabod rode like a demon for the bridge. He heard the black steed panting and blowing close behind him; he even fancied that he felt his hot breath. With a hard kick to poor Gunpowder, the horse sprang upon the bridge and thundered over the resounding planks. Gaining the opposite side, Ichabod cast an eye back to see if his pursuer should vanish, according to rule, in a flash of fire and brimstone. Just then he saw the goblin rising in his stirrups, and in the very act of hurling his head at him. Ichabod tried to dodge the horrible missile, but too late. It smashed into his head with a tremendous crash. He tumbled headlong into the dust, and Gunpowder, the black steed, and the goblin rider passed by like a whirlwind.

The next morning the old horse was found without his saddle at his master's gate. When Ichabod did not show at the schoolhouse, a search was called for. At the church bridge was found the hat of the unfortunate Ichabod, and close beside it a shattered pumpkin. But of Ichabod—nothing.

The brook was searched, but the schoolmaster was not to be discovered. The following Sunday much speculation was exchanged by the churchgoers. They shook their heads, and came to the conclusion that Ichabod had been carried off by the headless horseman. But some claimed he had fled town and lived in New York City, eventually rising to a position as Judge of the Courts. Brom Bones married the blooming Katrina the following year. It should be noted that many observed him to be exceedingly knowing whenever the story of Ichabod was related, and he always burst into a hearty laugh at the mention of the pumpkin. This led some to suspect that he knew more about the matter than he chose to tell. As for Ichabod, he was never seen again in Sleepy Hollow; but many swear that on a still summer evening, his voice can be heard chanting a melancholy psalm-tune far off in the distance hills.

THE MONKEY'S PAW

FROM THE TALE BY W. W. JACOBS

After the third glass of whiskey, the sergeant-major's eyes got brighter, and he began to talk of wars and plagues and strange people in even stranger lands. He had traveled the world over, and had only recently returned from India. Mr. White, with his wife and only son, Herbert, hung on the old soldier's every word.

"I'd like to go to India myself," said Mr. White, "just to look around a bit, you know. I should like to see those old temples and fakirs and jugglers. What was that you were telling me the other day about a monkey's paw or something you brought back?"

The sergeant-major set down his glass, and then took an odd-looking object from his pocket and set it on the table.

"This is a monkey's paw? Oh, my," said Mrs. White.

"Well, it's just a bit of what you might call magic, perhaps," said the sergeant-major gravely.

"What is there special about it?" asked Mr. White as he picked it up, examined it, and placed it again on the table.

"It had a spell put on it by an old fakir," the sergeant-major said, "a very holy man. He wanted to show that fate ruled people's lives, and that those who interfered with it did so to their sorrow. He put a spell on it so that three separate men could each have three wishes from it."

"Well, why don't you have three, sir?" said Herbert cleverly.

"I have," he said quietly, and his face paled as he spoke.

"And did your wishes come true?" asked Mrs. White.

"They did."

"And has anybody else wished?" asked Herbert.

"Yes. His first two wishes I do not know, but his third was for death. That's how I got the paw." And he suddenly picked up the paw and threw it into the fire. Mr. White hurriedly retrieved it from the fire before it burned.

"Better to have let it burn," said the sergeant-major. "If you keep it, don't blame me for what happens. If you must wish, wish for something sensible, or it will make you as sorry as I was."

After the sergeant-major left, the three began to talk.

"You don't really believe that fairy tale, do you?" asked Mrs. White with a smile.

"Well, it can't hurt to try. If it's a fake we're none the worse," said the son. "Go on, Father, wish for two hundred pounds."

"I suppose there's no harm in it. All right, I wish for two hundred pounds," said Mr. White as he held the paw in his hand. The next moment he dropped the paw, crying out. "It moved! I would swear that the thing moved in my hand!"

"Oh, don't be so silly," said Mrs. White. "All those stories have really got to you. I daresay you'll be up half the night."

When the two hundred pounds failed to show itself, the family decided it was time for bed. The paw was left on the table.

In the morning, Herbert went off to work at the factory as usual, and Mr. White, long retired, helped his wife around the house. That afternoon, a grave-looking man paid the Whites a visit. The stranger was brought into the parlor.

"I—was asked to call," he said slowly, then paused. "I come from Maw and Meggins, the factory."

"Is anything the matter?" said Mrs. White breathlessly. "Herbert? Oh, no! What is it, please?"

"I regret to inform you that your son was killed today. He came too close to the machinery and was dragged in. Though it can be of little comfort, the company has instructed me to give you the sum of *two hundred pounds* for the loss of your son."

Two weeks after the funeral the old couple's grief had not diminished. One night, while in bed, the wife cried out wildly, "*The paw?* The monkey's paw! Of course!"

"Where? What? What is it?" mumbled Mr. White, starting up from his sleep. "What's wrong?"

"Why didn't you think of it? The paw! We still have two wishes to make. Go get it, quickly!" his wife said excitedly.

"Was one not enough?" demanded the old man.

"No," she cried happily; "we'll have one more. Go down and get it, and wish our boy alive again!"

"You've gone mad! He has been two weeks in the grave, and besides he—I would not tell you, but—I could only recognize him by his clothing. If he was too terrible for you to see then, how now?"

"Bring him back," cried the old woman. "Do you think I fear the child I have nursed?" Dragging him downstairs, she put the paw in his hand and said, "*Wish!*"

No sooner had he made the terrible wish then a knock came at the door. There was another knock, and another. The old woman ran to the door and began undoing the locks.

"For God's sake don't let it in!" cried the old man, trembling.

"You're afraid of your own son," she said, struggling to reach the top bolt. The knocking grew louder and louder as she strained to reach the latch. "I can't reach the bolt! Help me!"

In his excitement, the old man had dropped the paw on the floor, and now he was on his hands and knees groping wildly in search of it. If he could only find it before the thing outside got in. The knocking now thundered throughout the house and was almost deafening. He heard the creaking of the bolt as it came slowly back, and at the same moment he found the paw, and frantically breathed his third and last wish. The knocking ceased suddenly, and he heard a long loud wail of misery from his wife as she ran out into the quiet, and now deserted, road.

The German Student

From The Tale By Washington Irving

On a stormy night in the time of the French Revolution, a young German student was returning to his lodgings in the old part of Paris. It was a very late hour as he made his way across the square where the public executions were held. The lightning quivered and clapped across the night sky, illuminating the guillotines that performed the bloody work.

The young man shrank back in horror at finding he was so close to these horrible instruments. His heart sickened at the thought of so many young and noble souls who had already perished at the hand of this Devil's tool. There they stood in grim array, amid a silent and sleeping city, awaiting fresh victims.

As he began to turn away from these grim reapers, he beheld a shadowy form cowering at the foot of the steps of one of the guillotines. A burst of lightning across the sky revealed it more distinctly. It was a woman, dressed all in black. She was seated on one of the lower steps, leaning forward, her face hidden in her lap. He paused. There was something awful in this solitary monument of woe. Here was some poor mourner, he thought, for whom the dreadful axe had taken all that was dear to her and left her without one reason to live.

He approached, and spoke in soothing tones to her. She raised her head to him and he was struck by her absolute beauty. Gathering himself together, he offered to conduct her to friends or family.

"I have no friend on earth!" she said.

"But you have a home," he insisted.

"Yes—in the grave!"

The heart of the student melted at these words.

Through kind and gentle words he finally persuaded her to come away with him and take shelter for the night in his apartment. He made up a bed for her and gave her a nightshirt to wear in place of her soaked dress. He was so fascinated by her charms, there seemed to be a spell upon his very thoughts and senses. She spoke no more of the guillotine. Her grief was gone.

He finally could contain himself no longer, and said, "You have no home or family. Let me be everything to you, or rather let us be everything to one another. I pledge myself to you forever!"

"Forever?" said the woman, solemnly.

"Forever!" he said, and he took her hand.

The next morning the student went to wake his newfound love. He spoke to her, but received no reply. On taking her hand, he found it cold—there was no pulse—her face was pallid and ghastly. In a word—she was a corpse.

Horrified and frantic, he summoned the police. As the police officer entered the room, he started back in terror on beholding the corpse.

"Great heaven!" he cried. "How did this woman come here?"

"Do you know anything about her?" the student asked eagerly.

"Do I?" exclaimed the police officer. "She was guillotined yesterday!"

He stepped forward, undid the black collar around the neck of the corpse, and the head rolled on the floor!

The student burst into a frenzy. "The fiend! The fiend has gained possession of me!" he shrieked. "I am lost forever!"

They tried to calm him, but in vain. He believed an evil spirit had tricked him out of his very soul. He went mad, and died shortly thereafter in an asylum.

THE JUDGE'S HOUSE

FROM THE TALE BY BRAM STOKER

When the time for his final examinations drew near Malcolm Malcolmson made up mind to go somewhere to read by himself. Wishing to avoid contact with friends that would certainly disturb his studies, he chose the town of Benchurch, a sleepy little town, as his escape. Upon arriving, he went straight to the one inn in town, and put up for the night.

The next day he set out to find even more isolated lodging than the inn afforded. There was only one place that took his fancy, and to most the word *desolation* would come to mind rather than *isolation* when referring to this place. It was an old rambling, heavy-built house that looked like it had not been lived in for decades. "Here," he thought, "is the very spot I have been looking for, and I should think I will be quite happy here."

He got the name of the agent in town, who was more than pleased to rent the home. It seemed there was some wild superstition surrounding the house, so the locals would have nothing to do with the place. He payed three months' rent in advance and then returned to the inn to gather his things.

Back at the inn, he told the landlady, who was kind and cheerful, of his plans to move into the house.

"Not the Judge's House!" she said, and she grew pale. "Oh, dear me! He was the Devil himself! He had many an innocent soul brought to the hangman for his wicked pleasure. They say the house is still haunted by his evil. Stay here, please, my boy."

But the student's mind was made up, so the landlady gathered provisions for him and found a caretaker to help him with his needs. In no time at all, the young student found himself comfortably situated within the great dining room of the house, as it was big enough for all his needs. A bed was brought in, food stored, and the room was throughly cleaned by the caretaker. By nightfall, he was alone, and happily began his studies.

He had been deeply immersed in his work for several hours when he first noticed the rats. How busy they were! Up and down behind the walls, over the ceiling and under the floor they raced, and gnawed, and scratched! At first they were a distraction, but after a while he grew accustomed to their wanderings, and gave them no further thought. That is, until they stopped.

It was near dawn when he suddenly became aware that a dread silence had fallen over the room. The rats had stopped. He looked up from his books and eyed the shadows about the room uneasily. The fire was low, but it still threw out a deep red glow.

His gaze fell upon something that sent chills running down his spine. There on the great high-backed carved oak chair by the right side of the fireplace sat an enormous rat, steadily glaring at him with baleful, wicked eyes. Those hateful eyes stirred him to anger, and he rose quickly to corner the intruder. Before he reached it, the rat, with a squeak that sounded like the pure concentration of hate, jumped upon the floor, and, running up the rope of the house alarm bell, disappeared into the darkness.

The student took up a lamp and went over to the corner of the room where the rat had disappeared. What he saw next set him to trembling. There, on the far wall, was a portrait of the Judge, sitting just as the rat had done, in the large oak chair. What had struck terror in the young man's heart were the eyes of the Judge. They were the same baleful eyes of the rat! From a tear in the upper part of the portrait, he saw the rat's head appear suddenly. He fell back in horror as the rat jumped from the portrait to the bell rope. He watched as the rat began to gnaw

furiously at the lower end of the rope, until he had bitten straight through. The rope fell with a thud to the floor. The rat ran back up the rope and jumped once again to the portrait. It was then that the *real* terror began.

In the center of the picture was a great patch of white canvas, as fresh as when it was stretched on the frame. The background was as before, with the chair and the rope, but the figure of the Judge had disappeared.

In a chill of horror, he beheld the Judge, who sat in the great high-backed carved oak chair in his robes of scarlet. The Judge glared vindictively, and a cruel, triumphant smile crossed his wicked face. In his hand he held an executioner's mask.

Slowly and deliberately the Judge rose from his chair and picked up the piece of the rope of the alarm bell that lay on the floor. He drew it through his hands as if he enjoyed its touch, and then began to fashion a noose. This he tightened, and he tested it with his foot until he was satisfied with its sturdiness. All the while he never once took his eyes off the cowering student. The noose now ready, the Judge placed the black hood over his head and moved slowly toward his helpless victim, who stood frozen, with his only movements being from his lips as he uttered low, whining whimpers of despair.

When the alarm bell of the Judge's House began to sound, a crowd soon gathered. Lights and torches of various kinds appeared, and soon a silent crowd was hurrying to the house. They knocked loudly at the door, but there was no reply. Then they burst in the door, and poured into the dining room, with the town doctor at the head.

There at the end of the rope of the great alarm bell hung the body of the student, and on the face of the Judge in the picture was a malignant smile.

THE BODY-SNATCHERS

FROM THE TALE BY ROBERT LOUIS STEVENSON

Every night in the year, at the Debenham Hotel, four of us sat in the bar and had drinks together—the undertaker, and the landlord, and Fettes, and myself. Sometimes there would be more; but blow high, blow low, come rain or snow or frost, we four would be there. Fettes was an old drunken Scotsman, a man of education obviously, and a man of some property, since he lived in idleness. He had come to Debenham years ago, while still fairly young, and of his past life he never talked.

One dark winter night the landlord was quite late arriving, due to the fact that one of the guests had fallen ill. The guest was a man of great wealth, and insisted on having his doctor from London attend him. The landlord had awaited the arrival of the doctor from London by the evening train.

"He's come," said the landlord, lighting his pipe.

"He?" said I. "Who?—not the doctor? What's his name?"

"Dr. Macfarlane," said the landlord.

Fettes was already through his third drink, and was fairly drunk; but at the last word he seemed to sober at once, saying, "Macfarlane? Where? Where is he?"

"Yes," said the landlord, "that's the name, Dr. Wolfe Macfarlane. Do you know him? Where are you going, Fettes?"

"I must see him face to face," is all Fettes would say as he left the bar.

"Toddy Macfarlane!" cried Fettes as he took the arm of the well-dressed and polished doctor.

The London doctor almost staggered. He stared at the man before him for a moment, glanced behind him with a sort of scare, and then in a startled whisper, "Fettes! You!"

"Ay," said the other, "me! Did you think I was dead, too? We are not so easy rid of our acquaintance."

"Hush, hush!" exclaimed the doctor. "This meeting is so unexpected. I really must be going, but we must do something for you, Fettes. I have money—"

"I don't want your blood money," Fettes said, clutching the doctor's arm tighter. "Tell me, Toddy, have you seen it again?"

At those words, the doctor pushed Fettes aside in frantic haste and made straight for his carriage. As what was later related to me that brought about this strange confrontation I shall try my best to narrate to you.

In his young days Fettes studied medicine in the schools of Edinburgh. He had a talent for his studies, and soon became a favorite of Dr. K—, the professor of anatomy. Fettes was placed in charge of the dissecting rooms and the dispensing of bodies for study. This required Fettes to sleep nights at the morgue, as bodies were often brought for sale in the wee hours of the morning.

Fettes would be awakened just before dawn by rough-looking fellows of low character. The body would be placed on the table, payment would be made, and no questions would be asked. As his boss would say, "Ask no questions for conscience's sake." And if it wasn't bad enough that he turned a blind eye to these late-night callers, he postively knew the harm of one of his other duties—grave robbing. When bodies were in short supply, he would go with his best friend, Dr. Wolfe Macfarlane, and steal a freshly buried corpse from a village graveyard.

So when he was awakened one dark night by Macfarlane, who placed a fresh body on the table, he should not have been surprised. But he was.

"What have you done? You've murdered this fellow!" he cried.

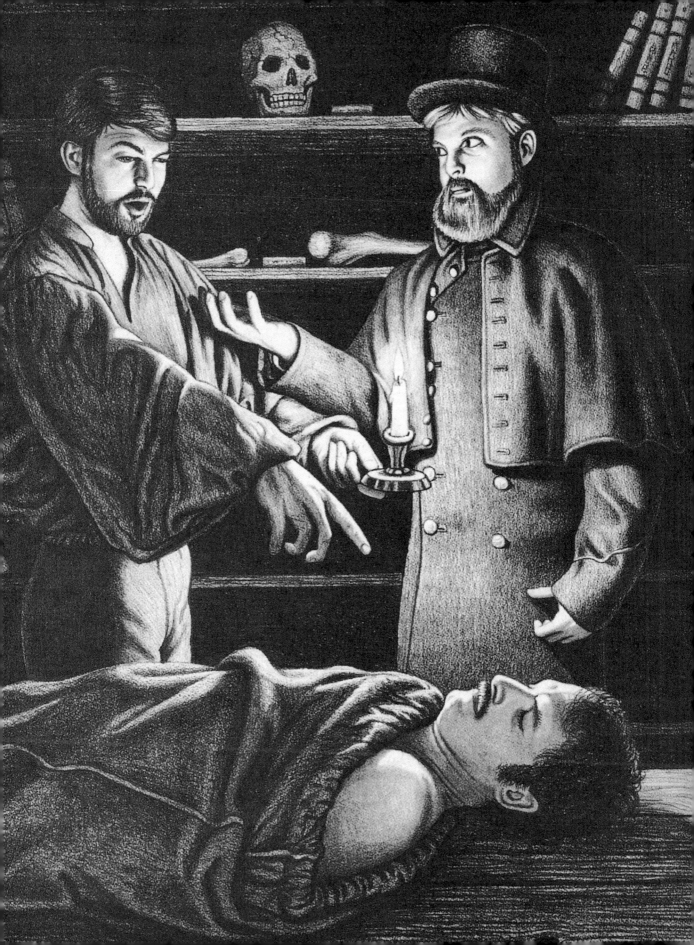

"I saw you having supper with him just last night! His name was Gray. Gray, that's it! He called you, Toddy, right? Why? How?"

"Do not concern yourself with the why and how, my friend, for now you need only to settle the account," Macfarlane said, holding out his hand for payment.

"Pay you?! Pay you for that!" Fettes cried.

"Why, yes. The books must be balanced. One body, one payment. Cheer up, there is nothing to be done. You won't say anything, of that I am sure, lest our midnight wanderings should become known."

Fettes knew he was right. Grave robbing was a serious crime. Fettes made the payment and tallied the book. The next day the body was dissected, including the head, and everything seemed all right. By week's end Fettes breathed a sigh of relief to find all was well.

The following week found the school once again short of bodies. Fettes and Macfarlane would have to make another midnight visit to a graveyard. They heard of a woman who had recently been laid to rest in a nearby village graveyard, and they set out by carriage on a stormy night to claim their prize.

It was pitch dark, but both were experienced with the wicked work, and in no time located the freshly made grave. A lantern was lit, and the two set about their ghoulish business. It was scarcely twenty minutes before they were rewarded by a dull rattle on the coffin lid. Bringing his spade back too sharply, Macfarlane knocked the lantern over and broke it. They had to complete their task in darkness. The coffin was exhumed and broken open; the body was placed in a sack and carried off to the carriage. With a crack of the whip, they were off.

The body had been placed between the two of them, and as they moved it would sway from side to side, bumping against each grave robber in turn. A creeping chill began to possess the soul of Fettes. He peered at the bundle, and it seemed somehow

larger than at first. All over the countryside, the farm dogs howled like demons at their passing. It grew and grew in his mind that some unnatural miracle had been accomplished, that some nameless change had befallen the dead body, and that it was in fear of their unholy burden that the dogs were howling.

"For God's sake," Fettes said, making a great effort at speech, "for God's sake, let's have a light!"

Seemingly Macfarlane was affected, too, and brought the carriage to a stop. Lighting a lamp, the two trembled with fear. The wet sack had molded to the outlines of the body underneath, the head was distinct from the trunk, the shoulders were plainly modeled. The two riveted their eyes on the ghastly comrade.

"That is not a woman," said Macfarlane, in a hushed voice.

"It was a woman when we put her in," whispered Fettes.

"Hold the lamp," said the other. "I must see her face."

And as Fettes took the lamp his companion untied the sack and drew down the cover from the head. The light fell very clearly upon the dark, well-molded features of a face they knew all too well. A wild yell rang out into the night; each leaped from his own side into the roadway. The lamp fell and went out. The horse, terrified by all the commotion, bounded and went off toward Edinburgh at a gallop, bearing along with it the sole occupant of the carriage, the body of the dead and long-dissected Gray.

Was It A Dream?

From The Tale By Guy de Maupassant

I had loved her madly!

Why does one love? How strange it is to see only one soul in the world, to have only one thought in one's mind, only one desire in the heart, and only one name on the lips. A name that one whispers ceaselessly, everywhere, like a prayer.

I met her and loved her, and then she died. She was buried! Buried! She! In that hole! At the head of her simple grave stood a white marble cross, with these few words:

"She loved, was loved, and died."

She is there below; how horrible! I sobbed for days before I could no longer bear the pain of my loss—our loss. I ran wildly through the streets, out of town. I ran to the graveyard where they had put her below. My only thought was to be by her side.

It was night. There was no moon. As I made my way through the graveyard in confusion, there came suddenly a bright glow from one of the tombstones. I froze in fright as a naked skeleton rose from the grave and turned to its stone, which read:

"Here lies Jacques Olivant, who died at the age of fifty-one. He loved his family, was kind and honorable, and died in the grace of the Lord."

The dead man picked up a small stone and began to scrape off the inscription. When this was done, he began to write with his bony finger in luminous letters, which read:

"Here lies Jacques Olivant, who died at the age of fifty-one. He hastened his father's death by his unkindness, as he wished to inherit his fortune; he tortured his wife, tormented his children, deceived his neighbors, robbed everyone he could, and died wretched."

When he had finished writing, the dead man stood motionless, looking at his work. Then all the dead rose up from their graves and began to write. And I saw that all had been the tormentors of their neighbors—malicious, dishonest, liars, thieves, rogues, and hypocrites! These good fathers, faithful wives, devoted sons, and pure daughters who were called irreproachable in life! They were all writing now, but this time it was the naked truth that marked their tombs.

I ran frantically through the dead to her grave to see what she had written. Where shortly before had read:

"She loved, was loved, and died."

I now saw:

"Having gone out in the rain one day, in order to deceive her lover, she caught cold and died."

It appears that they found me at daybreak, lying on the grave unconscious.